P9-DGV-808

The Blacker the Berry

Poems by
Joyce Carol Thomas

Illustrated by
Floyd Cooper

JOANNA COTLER BOOKS
An Imprint of HarperCollins*Publishers*
Amistad

Amistad is an imprint of HarperCollins Publishers.

The Blacker the Berry

For information address HarperCollins Children's Books, a division of HarperCollins Publishers, 1350 Avenue of the Americas, New York, NY 10019.
www.harpercollinschildrens.com

Library of Congress Cataloging-in-Publication Data
Thomas, Joyce Carol.
The blacker the berry / poems by Joyce Carol Thomas ;
illustrated by Floyd Cooper. — 1st ed. p. cm.
ISBN 978-0-06-025375-2 (trade bdg.) — ISBN 978-0-06-025376-9 (lib. bdg.)
1. African Americans—Juvenile poetry. [1. Children's poetry, American.
2. African Americans—Poetry. 3. American poetry.] I. Cooper, Floyd, ill.
PS3570.H565 B53 2008 96-26692
811'.54—dc20

Typography by Carla Weise
1 2 3 4 5 6 7 8 9 10
❖
First Edition

For Chrystal Pecot, with love
–J.C.T.

For Velma
–F.C.

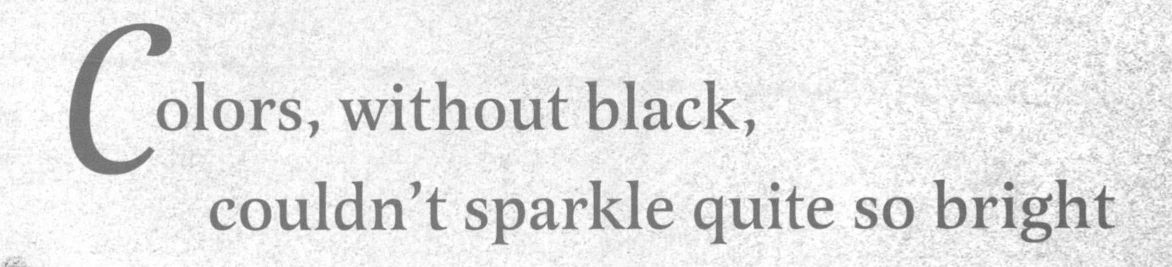

Colors, without black,
couldn't sparkle quite so bright

What Shade Is Human?

At breakfast
I pour milk all over my bowl of berries
And Grandpa says,
"It's the milk of kindness
    that makes us human."

"Yes, Papa," I answer,
    and he continues:
"White milk
Chocolate milk
Sweet milk
Mother's milk."

I nod between bites of berries
    because
My mother long ago
When she nursed me with first milk
Said, "You are beautiful."
And I heard her

The Blacker the Berry

"The blacker the berry
The sweeter the juice"

I am midnight and berries
I call the silver stars at dusk
By moonrise they appear
And we turn berries into nectar

Because I am dark the moon and stars
    shine brighter
Because berries are dark the juice is sweeter

Day couldn't dawn without the night
Colors, without black, couldn't sparkle
    quite so bright

"The blacker the berry
The sweeter the juice"

I am midnight and berries

Raspberry Black

I have been busy
Reading my great-great-grandmother's journal
How she loved the red earth
How she loved her pioneer-woman life
How she loved her Seminole Indian husband
How her children were African-Native-American
The color of black dipped in red

My mother says I am
Red raspberries stirred into blackberries
Like the raspberries I will always be here
Like the blackberries I was here
    from the first seed

I stay busy
Reading my great-great-grandmother's journal

I am African-Native-American
I am raspberry black

Golden Goodness

"Daddy, tell me this,
is yellow a good color?"

He says, "Go down yonder by the huckleberry bush
then come on back up here
and tell me what you see."

I mosey on out to the fruit vines
And pick the last basket of huckleberries

Then I notice the bronze on the summer leaves
turning to autumn

The bronze leaves of the berry bush
shine with a special light
And I look at my arms
And they are as bronze and golden
As the bush that gives good things

I run back into the house and tell Daddy,
"Daddy, Daddy, yellow is a good color!
Rich and bronze
And giving
Like me!"

Coffee Will Make You Black

"When I was your age," said Grandma,
"They used to say
'Coffee will make you black.'"

Why? I wondered

"Meant to keep certain colors down,"
she said

"But I fixed them," she said
"I ground the coffee berries
Each morning.

Then brewed them in a big old pot.

Then I sat at my table
And drank coffee so thick and black
A spoon could stand in it."

Cranberry Red

My skin is red
And my hair is red
"He's redder than a cranberry," they said
when I was born

Why am I red?

Maybe it's because I like cranberry sauce
With holiday dinners
Expecting me, Mama ate it every day

Maybe it's my Irish ancestors
Who reddened the Africa in my face
I don't know

My father's side of the family
Has hair as crinkly and red as mine
When we measure who we are
We don't leave anybody out
We count who we are
And add all who came before us
The way we figure it
We're just great

Sunshine Girl

Like a cat going
Round and round the mulberry bush
I follow the sunlight
From vine to vine
Instinctively following
What feels good

It feels absolutely fabulous
To be this brown
Anyway, I refuse to walk too long in shadow

Like the cat
It's against my nature

Biscuit Brown

I gather loganberries
From the trailing bush
Dancing prickly sweet
In my sunny backyard

I am biscuit brown
Brown as a biscuit
All warm and waiting
    for berries
        that I carry
            to the kitchen and can

When the berries in the jar
Are biscuit ready
I fix a cup of tea
Then spoon out biscuit jelly
For biscuit brown me

Skin Deep

"Beauty's only skin deep"
What did Grandma see
When she first looked in a mirror?

"Dear Heart," she says, "I gave you my soul,
in whatever color you're wearing now."

Is skin a dress
That's put on and changed
From life to life?

"You remind me of my mother
A long, long time ago," she says,
studying my beauty mark,
Her wrinkled hand holding my chin

"Put yourself in someone else's skin"

And I look into my own hazel eyes in the mirror
And see those sweet old folks at the age I am now
My great-grandma's raspberry color
My grandma's blackberry cheeks
And my mama's mulberry mouth

Night Shade

I feel as purple
As the night shade
Of an eggplant
That great berry among berries
Smooth skinned

And as stained and sweet
As my fingers
After rinsing boysenberries

Snowberries

I look white
I am as light
    as snowberries in fall

"I walk that walk
I talk that talk"

    Yet
Still some say
"You're not really Black!"

The words cut deep down
Beyond the bone
Beneath my snowy skin
Deep down where no one can see
I bleed the "one drop of blood"
That makes Black me

And I want to be as black
    as midnight
    and moonless water
So no words can wound me

Still I'm thankful
For all the blood drops I got
In my mind
Even one drop's a lot

Toast

The sun toasted me tan
Then chin in his hand
Sat back and admired his work

I am toasted wheat berry bread
Spread with melted butter

I am mango mellow
And gooseberry good

I am so toasty
The sun calls me
His toasty child

I am so toasty
I make the sun smile

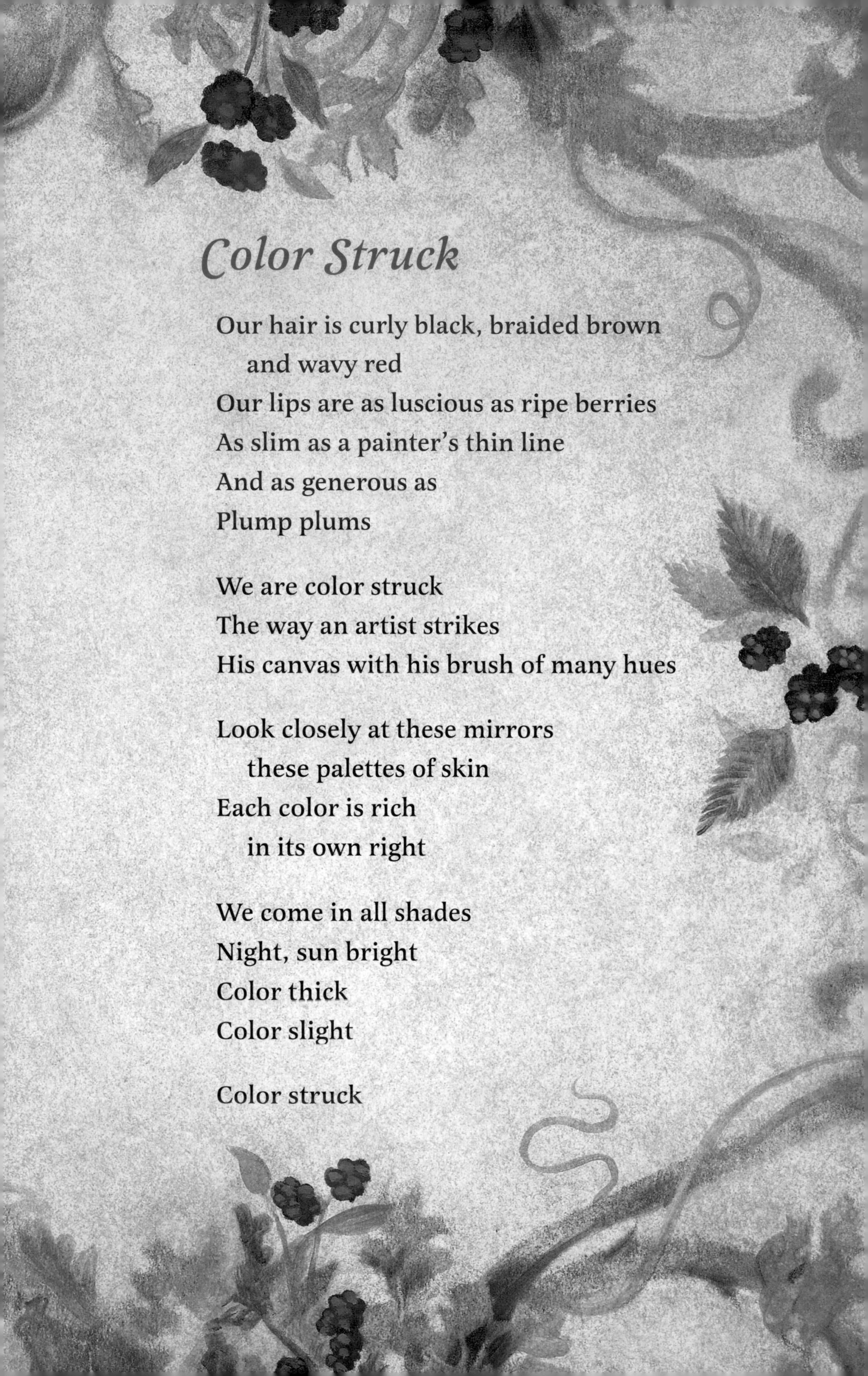

Color Struck

Our hair is curly black, braided brown
    and wavy red
Our lips are as luscious as ripe berries
As slim as a painter's thin line
And as generous as
Plump plums

We are color struck
The way an artist strikes
His canvas with his brush of many hues

Look closely at these mirrors
    these palettes of skin
Each color is rich
    in its own right

We come in all shades
Night, sun bright
Color thick
Color slight

Color struck